Growing Readers

Purchased with New Hanover County
Partnership for Children Funds

For Leroy

and his story

Also with love and thanks to my friends —

Tricia, Melanie,

Frank (especially for coediting late at night in Cork),

Carolyn, Kate, Helen,

Paul and Sybille,

and to Mark and Bonzo across the alleyway

Also to Cathryn

This story is based in and around
Salisbury Road and Beaumont Park,
Plymouth, England. Ordinary life.
Warmest thanks to Michaël Hill
and to Helen Read at Walker Books.

Copyright © 1997 by Simon James

All rights reserved.

First U.S. edition 1997

Library of Congress Cataloging-in-Publication Data

James, Simon.
Leon and Bob / Simon James.—1st U.S. ed.
Summary: Leon and his imaginary friend, Bob, do everything
together until a new boy moves in next door.
ISBN 1-56402-991-3
[1. Imaginary playmates—Fiction. 2. Friendship—Fiction.
3. Blacks—England—Fiction. 4. England—Fiction.] I. Title.
PZ7.J1544Le   1997
[E]—dc20   96-2684

10 9 8 7 6 5 4 3 2 1

Printed in Hong Kong

This book was typeset in Goudy.
The pictures were done in watercolor and ink.

Candlewick Press
2067 Massachusetts Avenue
Cambridge, Massachusetts 02140

LEON
AND
BOB

Simon James

CANDLEWICK PRESS
CAMBRIDGE, MASSACHUSETTS

Leon had moved into town
with his mom.
His dad was away in the army.
Leon shared his room
with his new friend, Bob.

No one else could see Bob,
but Leon knew he was there.
Leon always laid a place
for Bob at the table.
"More milk, Bob?" Leon said.

Sometimes Leon's mom
couldn't take Leon to school,
but Leon didn't mind.
He always walked to school with Bob.
He always had Bob to talk to.

Often, when Leon got home,
there was a letter waiting for him
from his dad.
Bob liked to hear Leon read it
over and over again.

One Saturday, Leon heard
some noises in the street below.
He saw a new family moving in
next door.
A boy looked up at Leon and waved.
Leon waved back.

That night Leon kept thinking
about the boy next door.
He decided to go by there
in the morning.
"But you'll have to come with
me, Bob," he said.

The next day Leon and Bob
ate their breakfast
very quickly.
Then Leon grabbed his ball
and rushed outside.

Leon ran up the steps
of the house next door.
He was about halfway
when suddenly he realized
Bob wasn't there anymore.

Leon sat down.

He was all alone.

He could ring the bell

or he could go home.

Why wasn't Bob there

to help him?

Leon rang the bell
and waited.
The door opened.
"Hello," said the boy.
"H-hello," said Leon.
"Would you like to go to the park?"

"Okay," said the boy.

"I'm just going to the park, Mom,"
he called.

Together Leon and the boy walked
down the steps toward the street.

"My name's Leon," said Leon.

"What's yours?"

"Bob," said Bob.